DORLING KINDERSLEY *READERS*

ROCKET RESCUE

Written by Nicola Baxter • Illustrated by Julian Baum

BEGINNING **2** TO READ ALONE

A Dorling Kindersley Book

Whoooosh!
As BB arrived at Space Port,
a rocket zoomed into the sky.
Lights flashed and
scientists hurried to their posts.

It was another busy day
at the space centre.

At the Training Station,
BB saw his teacher, Captain Walker.
"Are you ready for
your last day of training, BB?"
asked Captain Walker.
"Yes, Sir!" said BB.

Astronauts

Astronauts are people who fly into space. They must train and study for years before they make a flight.

He still couldn't believe
that he had won
the Space Port Competition.
Thousands of young people
had entered.
BB had come first.
He had won the
chance to train
as an astronaut.

BB had to pass one last test.
Then he could go
on a mission to Mars.
"This machine will show you what
it feels like to travel into space,"
Captain Walker told him.

BB climbed inside.
Suddenly, the machine started
spinning around, very, very fast.
BB felt strange and
his body felt light.
He was afraid he would be sick.

The machine stopped whizzing round.
At last, BB's head stopped spinning.
"You've passed the test, BB!"
said Captain Walker.
"Come with me to
Mission Control."

Training machine

Taking off in a rocket is bumpy and stressful! Astronauts train on a special machine, to get used to the feeling.

At Mission Control,
Captain Walker started talking to
Don Small, the Head Engineer.
BB looked at the computer screens.
An astronaut called Eena Orbit
was flying to the Moon.
The computers were following
her journey.

Suddenly, a light turned red!
"Captain Walker!" called BB.
"Something is badly wrong
with the Moon rocket!
Come and look at the computer!"

Don Small and Captain Walker
ran to look.

"Call a meeting!" said Don Small.

"Eena is in trouble.

We must act quickly!"

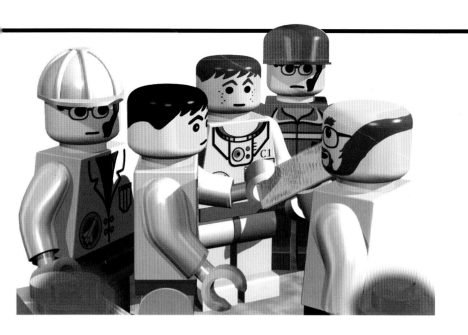

A few moments later,
all the Space Port scientists
were ready to help.
BB wanted to help, too.

Flight to the Moon
In 1969, astronauts
walked on the Moon
for the very first time.
They took off from
Earth in a rocket
as tall as a building!

Eena Orbit spoke over the radio.
"Please send help soon," she said.
"A meteor has hit the rocket."

"We must send two astronauts
to help Eena," Don Small said.
"We don't have much time."
"I'll go!" said Captain Walker.
"I can take off right away.
And BB is ready to be my co-pilot."
BB couldn't believe his ears.

Meteors

A meteor is a piece of rock, floating in space. It can cause lots of damage if it hits a spacecraft.

BB climbed into the space shuttle.
"Ready?" asked Captain Walker.

Take off

Powerful rockets carry a spacecraft into space. They use lots of fuel, because they must reach high speeds very quickly.

"Yes, Sir!" BB replied.

His mouth was dry.

His heart was beating fast.

Through his headphones,

he could hear Mission Control.

"Five,
four,
three,
two,
one..."

"Lift off!"

A white light filled the cabin
of the spacecraft.
The shuttle left the launch pad,
with a roar like thunder.
It shook and rattled
as it went faster and faster.
BB felt light and strange.
It was just like being
on the test machine.
But after only a few minutes,
the shuttle reached space and
the noise stopped.

"There's the rocket!"
said Captain Walker.
He spoke into his radio.
"Come in, Eena!"

Eena's voice was loud and clear.
"The meteor made a hole
in my rocket.
You must reach into the hole
to mend the computer.
I can't leave the controls."
"Are you ready for
your first space walk, BB?"
asked Captain Walker.
"Yes, Sir!" said BB.

Space walk
A space walk is when
an astronaut goes
outside a spacecraft,
to make repairs or
carry out experiments.

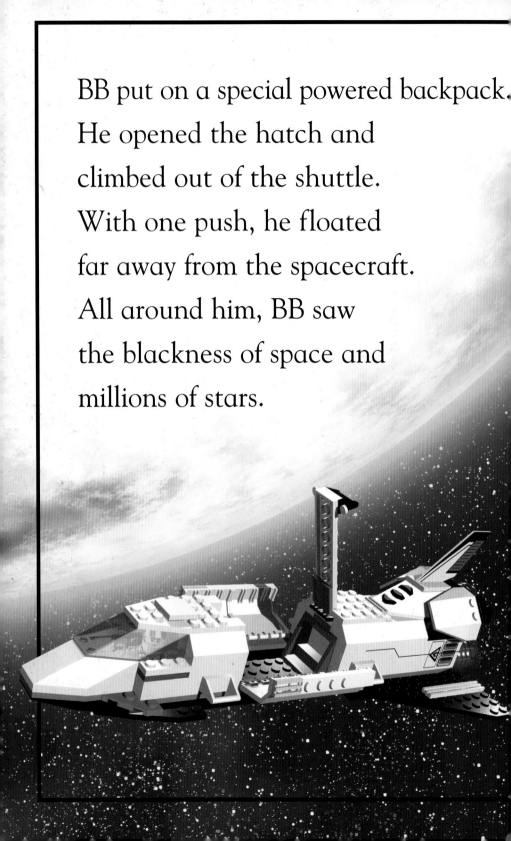

BB put on a special powered backpack.
He opened the hatch and
climbed out of the shuttle.
With one push, he floated
far away from the spacecraft.
All around him, BB saw
the blackness of space and
millions of stars.

Spacesuits

Astronauts wear special spacesuits to work outside their spacecraft. The suits keep them warm and help them breathe.

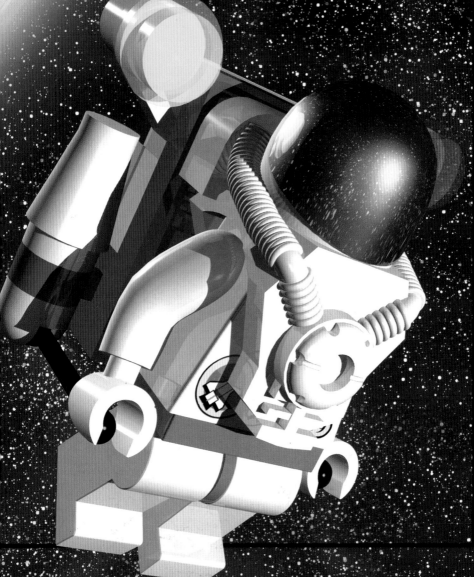

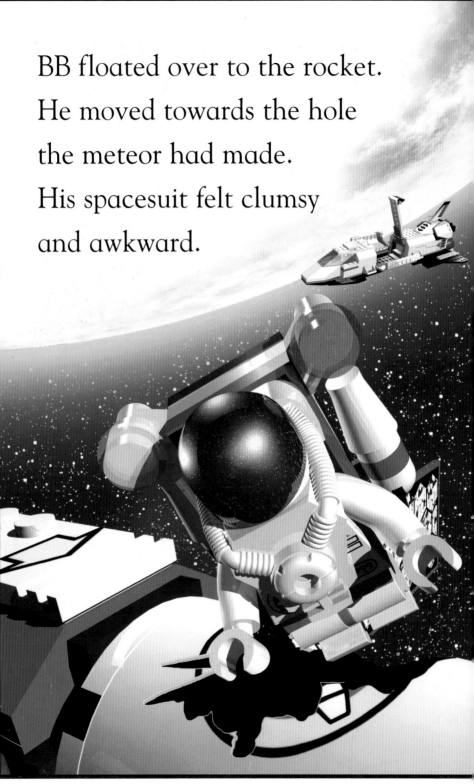

BB floated over to the rocket.
He moved towards the hole
the meteor had made.
His spacesuit felt clumsy
and awkward.

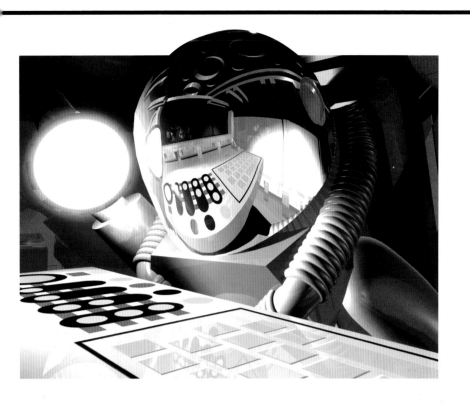

BB switched on his torch and
set to work on the computer.
Luckily, he had come top in
computer class at Space Port.
"How's it going?" Captain Walker
asked over the radio.
"I've fixed the computer," said BB.
"Now let's see if it works!"

BB pushed a switch and
held his breath.
Lights flickered on the screen.
The computer hummed.
It was working!
"You've done it!" said Eena Orbit.
"Well done!" said Captain Walker.

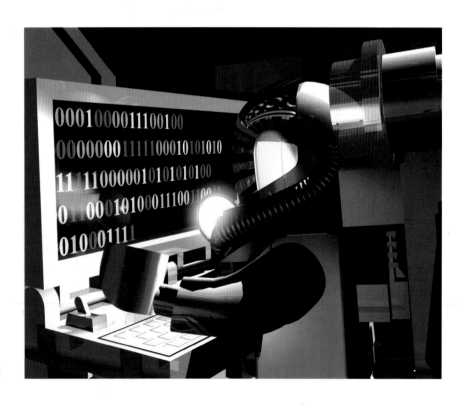

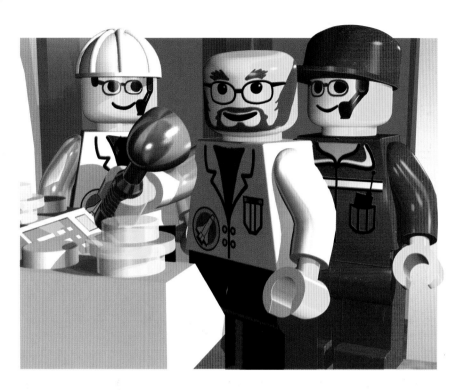

The scientists at Space Port
started to cheer.
The Moon Mission was saved!

Space travellers
More than 300 people
have travelled into space.
The astronauts have come
from the USA, Europe,
Russia and Japan.

Back in the shuttle,
BB gave a sigh of relief.
"I didn't think I could do it,"
he told Captain Walker.
"I knew you could!"
said Captain Walker.
"We knew it, too!"
called the Space Port scientists.

"Do you feel ready
for Mars, next time?"
asked Captain Walker.
"You bet, Sir!"
smiled BB.

Great space facts

Where is space?
Around the Earth, there is a 'blanket' of air, called the atmosphere. If we travelled into the sky, right up through the atmosphere, we would be in space.

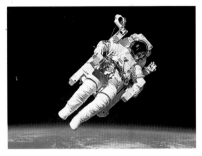

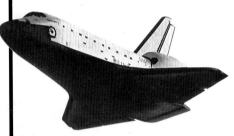

What is the difference between a rocket and a space shuttle?
A rocket can only be used once. Space shuttles can be used more than once.

What qualities does it take to be an astronaut?
Astronauts must be very good at science, and be physically fit, too.

How fast does a rocket go?
A rocket travels at around 28,000 kilometres per hour. A trip that would take six hours in an aeroplane takes about ten minutes in a rocket!

How long does a rocket take to get to the Moon?
About three days.